This book belongs to:

_____

To Nicholas

This paperback edition first published in 2013 by Andersen Press Ltd.,

20 Vauxhall Bridge Road, London SW1V 2SA.

Published in Australia by Random House Australia Pty.,

Level 3, 100 Pacific Highway, North Sydney, NSW 2060.

First published in Great Britain in 1987 by Andersen Press Ltd.

Copyright © David McKee, 1987.

Printed and bound in Singapore by Tien Wah Press.

10   9   8   7   6   5   4   3   2   1

British Library Cataloguing in Publication Data available.

ISBN 978 1 84939 763 6

THE SAD STORY OF
VERONICA
WHO PLAYED THE VIOLIN

Being an explanation of why the streets
are not full of happy dancing people

David McKee

Andersen Press

Veronica played the violin. At first she wasn't very good.
In fact, she was awful. Her first teacher left for China.

Her second teacher, Mrs Lionni, was deaf. Mrs Lionni read sad stories and said, "Very nice, dear, you just need to practise a lot."

Veronica did practise a lot because she was determined. It was terrible for the neighbours. "She is determined," they moaned.

The practice made Veronica play better, so she practised all the time.
"She is getting better," the neighbours wailed, "but she practises
all the time."

By the time her next birthday came, Veronica could
play really beautifully.
For her birthday, the whole family went on a picnic.

After tea, Veronica played the violin. It was her first concert.
The music she played was so beautiful that everyone cried
into their fizzy drinks.

Not long after that, Veronica's headmaster asked her why she never did any homework. "I have to practise the violin," said Veronica, and showed him.

"How beautifully sad," said the headmaster. "You must play at the school concert." Veronica played. That was her second concert.

At the concert was a famous music man. The next day he chased Veronica from school shouting that he would make her rich and famous.

Veronica left school to become a star. Soon her records were being played everywhere. It seemed as if she could make the whole world cry.

Veronica's most successful concert ended with a flood. In fact there was a storm at the time but Veronica and her music were given all the credit.

Then one day Veronica said, "Enough. All I've ever done is play the violin. I want adventure. I'm off to the deepest, darkest jungle."

"Oh, no, please, no," sobbed the music men.

Her mother wept too. "You'll be eaten alive," she cried – mothers always know best.
"Don't worry. My violin can calm the fiercest beast," smiled Veronica.

That afternoon she went to the safari park to prove it. Because she was famous the guards let her try. To their amazement, the lions just lay down and wept.

Veronica had proved her point and the following day her parents drove
her to the ship. They felt very sad as they waved her goodbye.

Veronica thought the voyage wonderful and at night she played beautifully sad music to the moon. The ship's pumps had to be kept going all the time.

When the ship landed, the men in uniform told Veronica, "You can't go into the jungle alone. You'll have to go with these fearless hunters or you'll be eaten alive."

"Okay," said Veronica.

For days Veronica and the fearless hunters marched through the jungle.

"Not so very exciting," thought Veronica.

She never once played her violin.

Then one afternoon, as they crossed a clearing, a tiger, a leopard and a lion appeared at the same time. At once the fearless hunters ran away, leaving Veronica alone.

Veronica wasn't at all worried.

Calmly, she took out her violin and began to play.

The animals stopped and listened but they didn't cry.

After days of not playing the music sounded different.
It was still beautiful, but now it was happy. The animals began
to dance and other animals arrived and joined in.

Soon the clearing was full of dancing animals. "Great," thought Veronica. "Enough of all that crying. When I get back, the streets will be full of happy, dancing people."

At that moment, from out of the jungle sprang an old lion.
With one giant bite, he ate Veronica.
She never even knew what had happened.

"What have you done?" cried the animals. "That was the most beautiful music we've ever heard."

The old lion put his paw behind his ear and said, "WHAT?"

All of which explains why the streets aren't full of happy, dancing people.

Other books by
David McKee

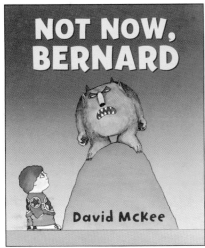

9781849394673

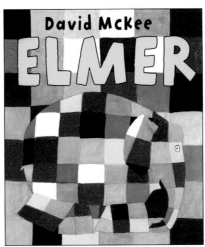

9781842707319

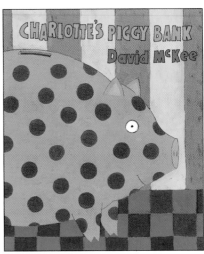

9781842703311

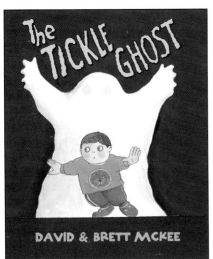

9781849392907

9781842704684

9781849393898